William Wordsworth

Woodsworth's Poems for the Young

William Wordsworth

Woodsworth's Poems for the Young

ISBN/EAN: 9783744712033

Printed in Europe, USA, Canada, Australia, Japan

Cover: Foto ©Andreas Hilbeck / pixelio.de

More available books at **www.hansebooks.com**

" We told o'er all that we had done,—
Our rambles by the swift brook's side."

CONTENTS.

CONTENTS.

LIST OF ILLUSTRATIONS.

LIST OF ILLUSTRATIONS.

THE PET LAMB.

THE dew was falling fast, the stars began to blink;
I heard a voice: it said, "Drink, pretty creature, drink!"

And, looking o'er the hedge, before me I espied
A snow-white mountain lamb, with a maiden at its side.

No other sheep were near, the lamb was all alone,
And by a slender cord was tethered to a stone;
With one knee on the grass did the little maiden kneel,
While to that mountain lamb she gave its evening meal.

The lamb, while from her hand he thus his supper took,
Seemed to feast with head and ears; and his tail with pleasure
  shook.
"Drink, pretty creature, drink," she said in such a tone,
That I almost received her heart into my own.

'Twas little Barbara Lewthwaite, a child of beauty rare!
I watched them with delight: they were a lovely pair.
Now with her empty can the maiden turned away;
But, ere ten yards were gone, her footsteps did she stay.

Towards the lamb she looked; and from that shady place
I, unobserved, could see the workings of her face:
If Nature to her tongue could measured numbers bring,
Thus, thought I, to her lamb that little maid might sing—

What ails thee, young one? What? Why pull so at thy cord?
Is it not well with thee? Well both for bed and board?

Thy plot of grass is soft, and green as grass can be;
Rest, little young one, rest: what is 't that aileth thee?

"What is it thou wouldst seek? What is wanting to thy heart?
Thy limbs, are they not strong? And beautiful thou art:
This grass is tender grass; these flowers they have no peers;
And that green corn all day is rustling in thy ears!

"If the sun be shining hot, do but stretch thy woollen chain,
This beech is standing by, its covert thou canst gain;
For rain and mountain storms! the like thou need'st not fear—
The rain and storm are things which scarcely can come here.

"Rest, little young one, rest; thou hast forgot the day
When my father found thee first in places far away:
Many flocks were on the hills, but thou wert owned by none,
And thy mother from thy side for evermore was gone.

"He took thee in his arms, and in pity brought thee home:
A blessed day for thee! Then whither wouldst thou roam?
A faithful nurse thou hast; the dam that did thee yean
Upon the mountain-tops no kinder could have been.

"Thou know'st that twice a day I have brought thee in this can
Fresh water from the brook, as clear as ever ran;
And twice in the day, when the ground is wet with dew,
I bring thee draughts of milk, warm milk it is, and new.

"Thy limbs will shortly be twice as stout as they are now,
Then I'll yoke thee to my cart, like a pony in the plough;
My playmate thou shalt be; and when the wind is cold,
Our hearth shall be thy bed, our house shall be thy fold.

"It will not, will not rest!—poor creature, can it be
That 't is thy mother's heart which is working so in thee?
Things that I know not of, belike, to thee are dear,
And dreams of things which thou canst neither see nor hear.

"Alas! the mountain-tops, that look so green and fair!
I've heard of fearful winds and darkness that come there;
The little brooks, that seem all pastime and all play,
When they are angry roar like lions for their prey.

"Here thou need'st not dread the raven in the sky;
Night and day thou art safe,—our cottage is hard by.
Why bleat so after me? Why pull so at thy chain?
Sleep—and at break of day I will come to thee again!"

As homeward through the lane I went with lazy feet,
This song to myself did I oftentimes repeat;
And it seemed, as I retraced the ballad line by line,
That but half of it was hers, and one-half of it was *mine*.

Again, and once again did I repeat the song;
"Nay," said I, "more than half to the *damsel* must belong.

For she looked with such a look, and she spake with such a
That I almost received her heart into my own."

ALICE FELL.

THE post-boy drove with fierce career,
  For threat'ning clouds the moon had drown'd;
When suddenly I seemed to hear
  A moan, a lamentable sound.

As if the wind blew many ways
  I heard the sound, and more and more:
It seemed to follow with the chaise,
  And still I heard it as before.

5

At length I to the boy call'd out,
　He stopp'd his horses at the word ;
But neither cry, nor voice, nor shout,.
　Nor aught else like it could be heard.

The boy then smack'd his whip, and fast
　The horses scamper'd through the rain ; ＼
And soon I heard upon the blast
　The voice, and bade him halt again.

Said I, alighting on the ground,
　"What can it be, this piteous moan ?"
And there a little girl I found,
　Sitting behind the chaise, alone.

"My cloak!"—the word was last and first,
　And loud and bitterly she wept,
As if her very heart would burst ;
　And down from off the chaise she leapt.

"What ails you, child?" She sobb'd, "Look here!"
　I saw it in the wheel entangled,—
A weather-beaten rag as e'er
　From any garden scarecrow dangled.

'T was fixed betwixt the nave and spoke ;
　Her help she lent, and with good heed
Together we released the cloak ;
　A wretched, wretched rag indeed!

C

"And whither are you going, child,
    To-night along these lonesome ways?"
"To Durham," answered she, half wild.
    "Then come with me into the chaise."

She sat like one past all relief;
    Sob after sob she forth did send
In wretchedness, as if her grief
    Could never, never have an end.

"My child, in Durham do you dwell?"
　　She check'd herself in her distress,
And said, "My name is Alice Fell;
　　I 'm fatherless and motherless.

"And I to Durham, Sir, belong."
　　And then, as if the thought would choke
Her very heart, her grief grew strong;
　　And all was for her tatter'd cloak.

The chaise drove on; our journey's end
　　Was nigh; and, sitting by my side,
As if she 'd lost her only friend,
　　She wept, nor would be pacified.

Up to the tavern door we post;
　　Of Alice and her grief I told;
And I gave money to the host
　　To buy a new cloak for the old.

"And let it be of duffil grey,
　　As warm a cloak as man can sell!"
Proud creature was she the next day,
　　The little orphan, Alice Fell!

FORESIGHT;

OR, THE CHARGE OF A CHILD TO HIS YOUNGER COMPANION.

THAT is a work of waste and ruin—
Do as Charles and I are doing!
　Strawberry-blossoms one and all,
We must spare them—here are many:
　Look at it—the flower is small,
Small and low, though fair as any;
Do not touch it!—summers two
I am older, Anne, than you.

C

Pull the primrose, sister Anne!
Pull as many as you can.
 — Here are daisies, take your fill;
Pansies and the cuckoo flower:
  Of the lofty daffodil
Make your bed and make your bower;
Fill your lap and fill your bosom;
Only spare the strawberry-blossom.

Primroses, the Spring may love them—
Summer knows but little of them;
  Violets, a barren kind,
Withered on the ground must lie;
  Daisies leave no fruit behind
When the pretty flow'rets die;

Pluck them, and another year
As many will be blowing here.

God has given a kindlier power
To the favoured strawberry-flower.

When the months of Spring are fled,
Hither let us bend our walk;

Lurking berries, ripe and red,
Then will hang on every stalk,

Each within its leafy bower;
And for that promise spare the flower!

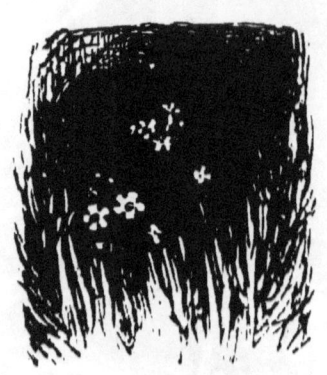

THE IDLE SHEPHERD-BOYS.

THE valley rings with mirth and joy;
  Among the hills the echoes play
A never, never-ending song,
  To welcome in the May;
The magpie chatters with delight;
  The mountain raven's youngling brood
Have left the mother and the nest,
And they go rambling east and west
  In search of their own food;
Or through the glittering vapours dart
In very wantonness of heart..

Beneath a rock, upon the grass,
  Two boys are sitting in the sun;
It seems they have no work to do,
  Or that their work is done.
On pipes of sycamore they play
  The fragments of a Christmas hymn;
Or with that plant which in our dale
We call stag-horn, or fox's tail,
  Their rusty hats they trim:

14

And thus, as happy as the day,
Those shepherds wear the time away.

Along the river's stony marge
The sand-lark chants a joyous song;

The thrush is busy in the wood,
  And carols loud and strong;
A thousand lambs are on the rocks,
  All newly born:—both earth and sky
Keep jubilee; and more than all,
Those boys with their green coronal;
  They never hear the cry,
That plaintive cry! which up the hill
Comes from the depth of Dungeon-Ghyll.

Said Walter, leaping from the ground,
  "Down to the stump of yon old yew
We 'll for our whistles run a race."
  ——Away the shepherds flew.
They leapt—they ran—and when they came
  Right opposite to Dungeon-Ghyll,
Seeing that he should lose the prize,
"Stop!" to his comrade Walter cries.
  James stopped with no good will:
Said Walter then, "Your task is here;
'T will keep you working half a year.

"Now cross where I shall cross—come on,
  And follow me where I shall lead."
The other took him at his word,
  But did not like the deed.

It was a spot which you may see
 If ever you to Langdale go:

Into a chasm a mighty block
Hath fallen, and made a bridge of rock:

The gulf is deep below;
And in a basin black and small
Receives a mighty waterfall.

With staff in hand across the cleft
  The challenger began his march;
And now, all eyes and feet, hath gained
  The middle of the arch.
When, list! he hears a piteous moan—
  Again!—his heart within him dies—
His pulse is stopped, his breath is lost,
He totters, pale as any ghost,
  And, looking down, he spies
A lamb, that in the pool is pent
Within that black and frightful rent.

The lamb had slipped into the stream,
  And safe without a bruise or wound
The cataract had borne him down
  Into the gulf profound.
His dam had seen him when he fell,
  She saw him down the torrent borne;
And, while with all a mother's love
She from the lofty rocks above
  Sent forth a cry forlorn,
The lamb, still swimming round and round,
Made answer to that plaintive sound.

When he had learnt what thing it was,
  That sent this rueful cry, I ween,
The boy recovered heart, and told
  The sight which he had seen.
Both gladly now deferred their task;
  Nor was there wanting other aid,—
A Poet, one who loves the brooks
Far better than the sages' books,
  By chance had thither strayed;
And there the helpless lamb he found,
By those huge rocks encompassed round.

He drew it gently from the pool,
  And brought it forth into the light;
The shepherds met him with his charge,
  An unexpected sight!
Into their arms the lamb they took:
  Said they, "He's neither maimed nor scarred."
Then up the steep ascent they hied,
And placed him at his mother's side;
  And gently did the Bard
Those idle shepherd-boys upbraid,
And bade them better mind their trade.

THE WATERFALL AND THE EGLANTINE.

" BEGONE, thou fond presumptuous elf !"
 Exclaimed a thundering voice,
" Nor dare to thrust thy foolish self
 Between me and my choice !"
A falling Water swoln with snows
Thus spake to a poor Brier Rose,
 That, all bespattered with his foam,
And dancing high, and dancing low,
Was living, as a child might know,
 In an unhappy home.

" Dost thou presume my course to block ?
 Off, off ; or, puny thing !
I 'll hurl thee headlong with the rock
 To which thy fibres cling."
The Flood was tyrannous and strong ;
The patient Brier suffered long,
 Nor did he utter groan or sigh,
Hoping the danger would be past ;
But, seeing no relief, at last
 He ventured to reply.

"Ah!" said the Brier, "blame me not;
  Why should we dwell in strife?

We who in this, our natal spot,
  Once lived a happy life!

You stirred me on my rocky bed—
What pleasure through my veins you spread!
  The Summer long, from day to day,
My leaves you freshened and bedewed;
Nor was it common gratitude
  That did your cares repay.

" When Spring came on with bud and bell,
    Among these rocks did I
Before you hang my wreaths, to tell
    That gentle days were nigh!
And in the sultry Summer hours,
I sheltered you with leaves and flowers;
  And in my leaves—now shed and gone—
The linnet lodged, and for us two,
Chanted his pretty songs, when you
    Had little voice or none.

" But now proud thoughts are in your breast—
    What grief is mine you see.
Ah! would you think, even yet how blest
    Together we might be!
Though of both leaf and flower bereft,
Some ornaments to me are left—
  Rich store of scarlet hips is mine,
With which I, in my humble way,

Would deck you many a Winter's day,
  A happy Eglantine !"

What more he said I cannot tell.
The Torrent thundered down the dell
  With unabating haste ;
I listened, nor aught else could hear ;
The Brier quaked—and much I fear
  Those accents were his last.

THE KITTEN AND THE FALLING LEAVES.

THAT way look, my infant, lo!
What a pretty baby show!
See the Kitten on the wall,
Sporting with the leaves that fall,
Withered leaves—one—two—and three—
From the lofty elder tree!

FOR THE YOUNG.

Through the calm and frosty air
Of this morning bright and fair,
Eddying round and round, they sink
Softly, slowly: one might think,
From the motions that are made,
Every little leaf conveyed
Sylph or fairy hither tending,
To this lower world descending,
Each invisible and mute,
In this wavering parachute.

——But the Kitten, how she starts,
Crouches, stretches, paws, and darts!
First at one, and then its fellow,
Just as light and just as yellow.
There are many now—now one—
Now they stop, and there are none.
What intenseness of desire
In her upward eye of fire!
With a tiger-leap half-way
Now she meets the coming prey;
Lets it go as fast, and then
Has it in her power again.
Now she works with three or four,
Like an Indian conjuror;
Quick as he in feats of art,
Far beyond in joy of heart.

Were her antics played in the eye
Of a thousand standers-by,
Clapping hands with shout and stare,
What would little Tabby care
For the plaudits of the crowd?
Over happy to be proud,
Over wealthy in the treasure
Of her own exceeding pleasure!

'T is a pretty baby treat,
Nor, I deem, for me unmeet;
Here, for neither babe nor me,
Other playmate can I see.
Of the countless living things,
That with stir of feet and wings
(In the sun or under shade,
Upon bough or grassy blade)
And with busy revellings,
Chirp and song, and murmurings,
Made this orchard's narrow space
And this vale so blithe a place,
Multitudes are swept away
Never more to breathe the day:
Some are sleeping; some in bands
Travelled into distant lands;
Others slunk to moor and wood,
Far from human neighbourhood;

And, among the kinds that keep
With us closer fellowship,
With us openly abide,
All have laid their mirth aside.
Where is he, that giddy sprite,
Blue-cap, with his colours bright,
Who was blest as bird could be,
Feeding in the apple tree;
Made such wanton spoil and rout,
Turning blossoms inside out;
Hung with head towards the ground,
Fluttered, perched, into a round
Bound himself, and then unbound;
Lithest, gaudiest Harlequin!
Prettiest tumbler ever seen!
Light of heart and light of limb,
What is now become of him?

Lambs that through the mountains went
Frisking, bleating merriment,
When the year was in its prime;
They are sobered by this time.
If you look to vale or hill,
If you listen, all is still,
Save a little neighbouring rill,
That from out the rocky ground
Strikes a solitary sound.

Vainly glitters hill and plain,
And the air is calm in vain;
Vainly morning spreads the lure
Of a sky serene and pure;
Creature none can she decoy
Into open sign of joy:
Is it that they have a fear
Of the dreary season near?
Or that other pleasures be
Sweeter even than gaiety?

Yet, whate'er enjoyments dwell
In the impenetrable cell
Of the silent heart which Nature
Furnishes to every creature;

FOR THE YOUNG.

Whatsoe'er we feel and know
Too sedate for outward show,
Such a light of gladness breaks,
Pretty Kitten! from thy freaks,—
Spreads with such a living grace
O'er my little Laura's face.

Yes, the sight so stirs and charms
Thee, baby, laughing in my arms,
That almost I could repine
That your transports are not mine,
That I do not wholly fare
Even as ye do, thoughtless pair!
And I will have my careless season
Spite of melancholy reason;
Will walk through life in such a way
That, when time brings on decay,
Now and then I may possess
Hours of perfect gladsomeness.
—Pleased by any random toy;
By a Kitten's busy joy,
Or an infant's laughing eye,
Sharing in the ecstasy;
I would fare like that or this,
Find my wisdom in my bliss;
Keep the sprightly soul awake,
And have faculties to take,

Even from things by sorrow wrought,
Matter for a jocund thought;
Spite of care and spite of grief,
To gambol with Life's falling leaf.

THE OAK AND THE BROOM.

His simple truths did Andrew glean
   Beside the babbling rills:
A careful student he had been
   Among the woods and hills.
One Winter's night, when through the trees
The wind was thundering, on his knees
   His youngest-born did Andrew hold;

And while the rest, a ruddy quire,
Were seated round their blazing fire,
This tale the shepherd told.

"I saw a crag, a lofty stone
    As ever tempest beat!
Out of its head an Oak had grown;
    A Broom out of its feet.
The time was March, a cheerful noon—
The thaw-wind, with the breath of June,
    Breathed gently from the warm south-west;
When in a voice sedate with age,
This Oak, a giant and a sage,
    His neighbour thus addressed:

"'Eight weary weeks, through rock and clay,
    Along this mountain's edge,
The frost has wrought both night and day,
    Wedge driving after wedge.
Look up! and think, above your head
What trouble, surely, will be bred.
    Last night I heard a crash—'t is true,
The splinters took another road—
I see them yonder—what a load
    For such a thing as you!

"'You are preparing, as before,
    To deck your slender shape;
And yet, three years back—no more—
    You had a strange escape.

32

Down from yon cliff a fragment broke ;
It came, you know, with fire and smoke,
   And hitherward it bent its way.
This ponderous block was caught by me,
And o'er your head, as you may see,
   'T is hanging to this day !

" 'The thing had better been asleep,
   Whatever thing it were,
Or breeze, or bird, or dog, or sheep,
   That first did plant you there.
For you and your green twigs decoy
The little witless shepherd-boy
   To come and slumber in your bower ;
And, trust me, on some sultry noon,
Both you and he, Heaven knows how soon !
   Will perish in one hour.

" ' From me this friendly warning take.'—
   The Broom began to doze,
And thus, to keep herself awake,
   Did gently interpose :
' My thanks for your discourse are due ;
That it is true, and more than true,
   I know, and I have known it long :
Frail is the bond by which we hold
Our being, be we young or old,
   Wise, foolish, weak, or strong.

" ' Disasters, do the best we can,
   Will reach both great and small;
And he is oft the wisest man
   Who is not wise at all.
For me, why should I wish to roam?
This spot is my paternal home;
   It is my pleasant heritage.
My father, many a happy year,
Here spread his careless blossoms, here
   Attained a good old age.

" ' Even such as his may be my lot.
   What cause have I to haunt
My heart with terrors? Am I not,
   In truth, a favoured plant?
On me such bounty Summer pours,
That I am covered o'er with flowers;
   And, when the frost is in the sky,
My branches are so fresh and gay,
That you might look at me and say,
   That plant can never die.

" ' The butterfly, all green and gold,
   To me hath often flown,
Here in my blossoms to behold
   Wings lovely as his own.

When grass is chill with rain or dew,
Beneath my shade the mother ewe
   Lies with her infant lamb; I see
The love they to each other make,
And the sweet joy which they partake,
   It is a joy to me.'

"Her voice was blithe, her heart was light;
   The Broom might have pursued
Her speech until the stars of night
   Their journey had renewed;
But in the branches of the Oak
Two ravens now began to croak
   Their nuptial song—a gladsome air;
And to her own green bower the breeze
That instant brought two stripling bees,
   To rest and murmur there.

"One night, my children, from the north,
   There came a furious blast.
At break of day I ventured forth,
   And near the cliff I passed.
The storm had fallen upon the Oak,
And struck him with a mighty stroke,
   And whirled, and whirled him far away;
And, in one hospitable cleft,

35

The little careless Broom was left
To live for many a day."

THE MOTHER'S RETURN.

A MONTH, sweet little ones, is passed
   Since your dear mother went away;
And she to-morrow will return:
   To-morrow is the happy day.

O blessed tidings! thought of joy!
   The eldest heard with steady glee.
Silent he stood; then laughed amain,
   And shouted, "Mother, come to me!"

Louder and louder did he shout,
   With witless hope to bring her near.
"Nay, patience! patience, little boy!
   Your tender mother cannot hear."

I told of hills and far-off towns,
   And long, long vales to travel through —
He listens, puzzled, sore perplexed;
   But he submits — what can he do?

No strife disturbs his sister's breast;
   She wars not with the mystery
Of time and distance, night and day,
   The bonds of our humanity.

Her joy is like an instinct — joy
   Of kitten, bird, or Summer fly;
She dances, runs without an aim,
   She chatters in her ecstasy.

Her brother now takes up the note,
   And echoes back his sister's glee;
They hug the infant in my arms,
   As if to force his sympathy.

37

Then settling into fond discourse,
  We rested in the garden bower,
While sweetly shone the evening sun
  In his departing hour.

We told o'er all that we had done —
 ' Our rambles by the swift brook's side,
Far as the willow-skirted pool,   '
  Where two fair swans together glide.

We talked of change, of winter gone,
Of green leaves on the hawthorn spray,

Of birds that build their nests and sing,
And "all since Mother went away!"

39

To her these tales they will repeat,
　To her our new-born tribes will show,
The goslings green, the ass's colt,
　The lambs that in the meadow go.

But see, the evening star comes forth!
　To bed the children must depart:
A moment's heaviness they feel,
　A sadness at the heart.

'Tis gone — and in a merry fit
    They run upstairs in gamesome race;
I too, infected by their mood,
    I could have joined the wanton chase.

Five minutes past — and, oh, the change! —
    Asleep upon their beds they lie;
Their busy limbs in perfect rest,
    And closed the sparkling eye.

G

ADDRESS TO A CHILD, DURING A BOISTEROUS WINTER EVENING.

WHAT way does the wind come? What way does he go?
He rides over the water, and over the snow,
Through wood, and through vale; and o'er rocky height
Which the goat cannot climb, takes his sounding flight.

He tosses about in every bare tree,
As, if you look up, you plainly may see;
But how he will come, and whither he goes,
There's never a scholar in England knows.

He will suddenly stop in a cunning nook,
And ring a sharp 'larum; but if you should look,
There's nothing to see but a cushion of snow
Round as a pillow, and whiter than milk,
And softer than if it were covered with silk.

Sometimes he'll hide in the cave of a rock,
The whistle as shrill as a buzzard cock;
—Yet seek him—and what shall you find in the place?
Nothing but silence and empty space,

Save, in a corner, a heap of dry leaves
That he's left for a bed for beggars or thieves!

As soon as 'tis daylight, to-morrow with me
You shall go to the orchard, and then you will see

That he has been there, and made a great rout,
And cracked the branches, and strown them about.
Heaven grant that he spare but that one upright twig
That looked up to the sky so proud and big
All last Summer, as well you know,
Studded with apples, a beautiful show!
Hark! over the roof he makes a pause,
And growls as if he would fix his claws
Right in the slates, and with a huge rattle
Drive them down, like men in a battle:

—But let him range round; he does us no harm:
We build up the fire, we're snug and warm;
Untouch'd by his breath, see, the candle shines bright,
And burns with a clear and steady light;
Books have we to read,—hush!—that half-stifled knell,
Methinks 't is the sound of the eight o'clock bell.

—Come, now we'll to bed; and when we are there
He may work his own will, and what shall we care?
He may knock at the door,—we'll not let him in;
May drive at the windows,—we'll laugh at his din:
Let him seek his own home wherever it be;
Here's a *cozie* warm house for Edward and me.

POOR SUSAN.

At the corner of Wood Street, when daylight appears,
There's a thrush that sings loud, it has sung for three years;
Poor Susan has passed by the spot, and has heard
In the silence of morning the song of the bird.

'Tis a note of enchantment: what ails her?   She sees
A mountain ascending, a vision of trees;
Bright volumes of vapour through Lothbury glide,
And a river flows on through the vale of Cheapside.

Green pastures she views in the midst of the dale,
Down which she so often has tripped with her pail;
And a single small cottage, a nest like a dove's,
The one only dwelling on earth that she loves.

She looks, and her heart is in heaven: but they fade,
The mist and the river, the hill and the shade:
The stream will not flow, and the hill will not rise,
And the colours have all passed away from her eyes.

WE ARE SEVEN.

     A simple child
  That lightly draws its breath,
And feels its life in every limb,
  What should it know of death?

I met a little cottage girl:
  She was eight years old, she said;
Her hair was thick with many a curl
  That clustered round her head.

She had a rustic, woodland air,
  And she was wildly clad;
Her eyes were fair, and very fair;
  —Her beauty made me glad.

"Sisters and brothers, little maid,
  How many may you be?"
"How many? Seven in all," she said,
  And wondering looked at me.

"And where are they? I pray you tell."
  She answered, "Seven are we;
And two of us at Conway dwell,
  And two are gone to sea.

"Two of us in the churchyard lie,
  My sister and my brother;
And, in the churchyard cottage, I
  Dwell near them with my mother."

"You say that two at Conway dwell,
  And two are gone to sea,
Yet ye are seven!—I pray you tell,
  Sweet maid, how this may be?"

Then did the little maid reply,
  "Seven boys and girls are we;
Two of us in the churchyard lie,
  Beneath the churchyard tree."

"You run about, my little maid,
   Your limbs they are alive;
If two are in the churchyard laid,
   Then ye are only five."

"Their graves are green, they may be seen,"
   The little maid replied,
"Twelve steps or more from my mother's door,
   And they are side by side.

"My stockings there I often knit,
  My kerchief there I hem;
And there upon the ground I sit—
  I sit and sing to them.

"And often after sunset, Sir,
  When it is light and fair,
I take my little porringer,
  And eat my supper there.

"The first that died was little Jane;
  In bed she moaning lay,
Till God released her of her pain,
  And then she went away.

"So in the churchyard she was laid;
  And all the Summer dry,
Together round her grave we played,
  My brother John and I.

"And when the ground was white with snow
  And I could run and slide,
My brother John was forced to go,
  And he lies by her side."

"How many are you, then," said I,
  "If they two are in heaven?"
The little maiden did reply,
  "O master! we are seven."

"But they are dead; these two are dead!
    Their spirits are in heaven!"
'Twas throwing words away; for still
The little maid would have her will,
    And said, "Nay, we are seven!"

FIDELITY.

A BARKING sound the shepherd hears,
   A cry as of a dog or fox;
He halts, and searches with his eyes
   Among the scattered rocks:
And now at distance can discern
A stirring in a break of fern;
And instantly a dog is seen,
Glancing from that covert green.

The dog is not of mountain breed;
   Its motions, too, are wild and shy;
With something, as the shepherd thinks,
   Unusual in its cry:
Nor is there any one in sight
All round, in hollow or on height;
Nor shout nor whistle strikes his ear:
What is the creature doing here?

It was a cove, a huge recess,
   That keeps, till June, December's snow;
A lofty precipice in front,
   A silent tarn below!

Far in the bosom of Helvellyn,
Remote from public road or dwelling,
Pathway, or cultivated land,
From trace of human foot or hand.

There sometimes doth a leaping fish
  Send through the tarn a lonely cheer;
The crags repeat the raven's croak,
  In symphony austere;
Thither the rainbow comes—the cloud—
And mists that spread the flying shroud;
And sunbeams; and the sounding blast,
That, if it could, would hurry past,
But that enormous barrier binds it fast.

Not free from boding thoughts, awhile
  The shepherd stood; then makes his way
Towards the dog, o'er rocks and stones,
  As quickly as he may;
Nor far had gone before he found
A human skeleton on the ground:
The appalled discoverer with a sigh
Looks round to learn the history.

From those abrupt and perilous rocks
  The man had fallen, that place of fear!
At length upon the shepherd's mind
  It breaks, and all is clear:

He instantly recalled the name,
And who he was, and whence he came;
Remembered, too, the very day
On which the traveller passed this way.

But hear a wonder, for whose sake
  This lamentable tale I tell!
A lasting monument of words
  This wonder merits well.
The dog which still was hovering nigh,
Repeating the same timid cry,
This dog had been through three months' space
A dweller in that savage place.

Yes, proof was plain that since the day
  On which the traveller thus had died
The dog had watched about the spot,
  Or by his master's side:
How nourished here through such long time
He knows who gave that love sublime,
And gave that strength of feeling great
Above all human estimate.

TO A BUTTERFLY.

Stay near me—do not take thy flight!
A little longer stay in sight!
Much converse do I find in thee,
Historian of my infancy!

Float near me; do not yet depart!
  Dead times revive in thee:
Thou bring'st, gay creature as thou art!
A solemn image to my heart,
  My father's family!

Oh! pleasant, pleasant were the days,
The time when, in our childish plays,
My sister Emmeline and I
Together chased the butterfly!
A very hunter did I rush
  Upon the prey:—with leaps and springs
I followed on from brake to bush;
But she, God love her! feared to brush
  The dust from off its wings.

.

GOODY BLAKE AND HARRY GILL.

A TRUE STORY.

Oh! what's the matter? what's the matter?
  What is 't that ails young Harry Gill,
That evermore his teeth they chatter,
  Chatter, chatter, chatter still?
Of waistcoats Harry has no lack,
  Good duffil grey, and flannel fine;
He has a blanket on his back,
  And coats enough to smother nine.

In March, December, and in July,
  'T is all the same with Harry Gill:
The neighbours tell, and tell you truly,
  His teeth they chatter, chatter still,
At night, at morning, and at noon,—
  'T is all the same with Harry Gill;
Beneath the sun, beneath the moon,
  His teeth they chatter, chatter still!

Young Harry was a lusty drover,
  And who so stout of limb as he?
His cheeks were red as ruddy clover;
  His voice was like the voice of three.
Old Goody Blake was old and poor;
  Ill-fed she was, and thinly clad;
And any man who passed her door
  Might see how poor a hut she had.

All day she spun in her poor dwelling;
  And then her three hours' work at night!
Alas! 'twas hardly worth the telling,
  It would not pay for candle-light.
This woman dwelt in Dorsetshire,—
  Her hut was on a cold hill-side,
And in that country coals are dear,
  For they come far by wind and tide.

By the same fire to boil their pottage
  Two poor old dames, as I have known,
Will often live in one small cottage;
  But she, poor woman! dwelt alone.
'Twas well enough when Summer came,
  The long, warm, lightsome Summer day,
Then at her door the *canty* dame
  Would sit, as any linnet gay.

But when the ice our streams did fetter,
  Oh, then how her old bones would shake!
You would have said, if you had met her,
  'Twas a hard time for Goody Blake.
Her evenings then were dull and dead:
  Sad case it was, as you may think,
For very cold to go to bed,
  And then for cold not sleep a wink.

Oh, joy for her! whene'er in Winter
  The winds at night had made a rout,
And scattered many a lusty splinter
  And many a rotten bough about.
Yet never had she, well or sick,
  As every man who knew her says,
A pile beforehand, wood or stick,
  · Enough to warm her for three days.

Now, when the frost was past enduring,
  And made her poor old bones to ache,
Could anything be more alluring
  Than an old hedge to Goody Blake?
And, now and then, it must be said,
  When her old bones were cold and chill,
She left her fire, or left her bed,
  To seek the hedge of Harry Gill.

Now Harry he had long suspected
  This trespass of old Goody Blake;
And vowed that she should be detected,
  And he on her would vengeance take.
And oft from his warm fire he 'd go,
  And to the fields his road would take;
And there, at night, in frost and snow,
  He watched to seize old Goody Blake.

And once behind a rick of barley
  Thus looking out did Harry stand:
The moon was full and shining clearly,
  And crisp with frost the stubble land.
—He hears a noise—he 's all awake—
  Again!—on tip-toe down the hill
He softly creeps—'t is Goody Blake!
  She 's at the hedge of Harry Gill!

Right glad was he when he beheld her:
  Stick after stick did Goody pull:
He stood behind a bush of elder,
  Till she had filled her apron full.
When with her load she turned about,
  The bye-road back again to take,
He started forward with a shout,
  And sprang upon poor Goody Blake.

And fiercely by the arm he took her,
 And by the arm he held her fast,
And fiercely by the arm he shook her,
 And cried, "I 've caught you, then, at last!"
Then Goody, who had nothing said,
 Her bundle from her lap let fall;
And, kneeling on the sticks, she prayed
 To God that is the Judge of all.

She prayèd, her withered hand uprearing,
 While Harry held her by the arm—
"God! who art never out of hearing,
 Oh may he never more be warm!"
The cold, cold moon above her head,
 Thus on her knees did Goody pray;
Young Harry heard what she had said,
 And icy cold he turned away.

He went complaining all the morrow
 That he was cold and very chill:
His face was gloom, his heart was sorrow,
 Alas! that day, for Harry Gill!
That day he wore a riding-coat,
 But not a whit the warmer he;
Another was on Thursday brought,
 And ere the Sabbath he had three.

'T was all in vain, a useless matter,—
　And blankets were about him pinned;
Yet still his jaws and teeth they clatter,
　Like a loose casement in the wind.
And Harry's flesh it fell away;
　And all who see him say, 'T is plain
That, live as long as live he may,
　He never will be warm again.

No word to any man he utters,
　Abed or up, to young or old;
But ever to himself he mutters,
　"Poor Harry Gill is very cold."
Abed or up, by night or day,
　His teeth they chatter, chatter still.
Now think, ye farmers all, I pray,
　Of Goody Blake and Harry Gill.

THE SPARROW'S NEST.

BEHOLD, within the leafy shade,
Those bright blue eyes together laid!
On me the chance-discovered sight
Gleamed like a vision of delight.—

I started—seeming to espy
  The home and sheltered bed,—
The Sparrow's dwelling, which, hard by
My father's house, in wet or dry,
My sister Emmeline and I
  Together visited.

She looked at it as if she feared it;
Still wishing, dreading to be near it:
Such heart was in her, being then
A little prattler among men.
The blessing of my latter years
  Was with me when a boy:
She gave me eyes, she gave me ears;
And humble cares, and delicate fears;
A heart, the fountain of sweet tears,
  And love, and thought, and joy.

THE LAST OF THE FLOCK.

In distant countries have I been,
And yet I have not often seen
A healthy man, a man full-grown,
Weep in the public roads alone.
But such a one on English ground,
  And in the broad highway, I met.
Along the broad highway he came,
  His cheeks with tears were wet.
Sturdy he seemed, though he was sad;
And in his arms a lamb he had.
He saw me, and he turned aside,
As if he wished himself to hide;
Then with his coat he made essay
To wipe those briny tears away.
I followed him, and said, "My friend,
  What ails you? — wherefore weep you so?"
"Shame on me, Sir! this lusty lamb,
  He makes my tears to flow.
To-day I fetched him from the rock;
He is the last of all my flock.

When I was young, a single man,
And after youthful follies ran,
Though little given to care and thought,
Yet, so it was, a ewe I bought;
And other sheep, from her I raised,
    As healthy sheep as you might see;
And then I married, and was rich
    As I could wish to be;
Of sheep I numbered a full score,
And every year increased my store.
Year after year my stock it grew;
And from this one, this single ewe,
Full fifty comely sheep I raised,
As sweet a flock as ever grazed.
Upon the mountain did they feed,—
    They throve, and we at home did thrive.
—This lusty lamb, of all my store,
    Is all that is alive;
' And now I care not if we die,
And perish all of poverty.

"Six children, Sir, had I to feed,—
Hard labour in a time of need!
My pride was tamed, and in our grief
I of the parish asked relief.
They said I was a wealthy man,

My sheep upon the mountain fed,
And it was fit that thence I took
  Whereof to buy us bread.
'Do this: how can we give to you,'
  They cried, 'what to the poor is due?'

"I sold a sheep, as they had said,
And bought my little children bread,
And they were healthy with their food;
For me—it never did me good.
A woeful time it was for me,
  To see the end of all my gains,
The pretty flock which I had reared
  With all my care and pains,
To see it melt like snow away!
For me it was a woeful day.

"Another still! and still another!
A little lamb, and then its mother!
It was a vein that never stopped—
Like blood-drops from my heart they dropped,
Till thirty were not left alive.
  They dwindled, dwindled, one by one;
And I may say that many a time
  I wished they all were gone:
They dwindled one by one away!
For me it was a woeful day.

"To wicked deeds I was inclined,
And wicked fancies crossed my mind;
And every man I chanced to see,
I thought he knew some ill of me.
No peace, no comfort could I find,
No ease within doors or without;
And crazily and wearily
I went my work about.
Ofttimes I thought to run away!
For me it was a woeful day.

"Sir, 't was a precious flock to me,
As dear as my own children be;
For daily with my growing store
I loved my children more and more.
Alas! it was an evil time:
God cursed me in my sore distress.
I prayed, yet every day I thought
I loved my children less;
And every week and every day,
My flock it seemed to melt away.

"They dwindled, Sir,—sad sight to see!—
From ten to five, from five to three—
A lamb, a wether, and a ewe—
And then, at last, from three to two;
And of my fifty, yesterday

I had but only one;
And here it lies upon my arm,
    Alas! and I have none —
To-day I fetched it from the rock;
It is the last of all my flock."

THE REDBREAST AND THE BUTTERFLY.

Art thou the bird whom man loves best,
The pious bird with the scarlet breast,

Our little English Robin;
The bird that comes about our doors
　When Autumn winds are sobbing?
Art thou the Peter of Norway boors?
　Their Thomas in Finland,
　And Russia far inland?
The bird whom, by some name or other,
All men who know thee call their brother,
　The darling of children and men?
Could Father Adam * open his eyes,
And see this sight beneath the skies,
　He'd wish to close them again.

If the Butterfly knew but his friend,
Hither his flight he would bend;
And find his way to me.
Under the branches of the tree,
In and out, he darts about:
　Can this be the bird, to man so good,
That, after their bewildering,
Did cover with leaves the little Children
　So painfully in the Wood?

* "Paradise Lost," Book XI., where Adam points out to Eve the
ominous sign of the eagle chasing "two birds of gayest plume,"
and the gentle hart and hind pursued by their enemy.

What ailed thee, Robin, that thou could'st pursue
   A beautiful creature,
   That is gentle by nature?
Beneath the Summer sky
From flower to flower let him fly;
'T is all that he wishes to do.
The cheerer thou of our in-door sadness,
He is the friend of our Summer gladness:
What hinders, then, that you should be
Playmates in the sunny weather,
And fly about in the air together?
His beautiful wings in crimson are drest,
   A crimson as bright as thine own:
If thou would'st be happy in thy nest,
O pious bird whom man loves best,
   Love him, or leave him alone.

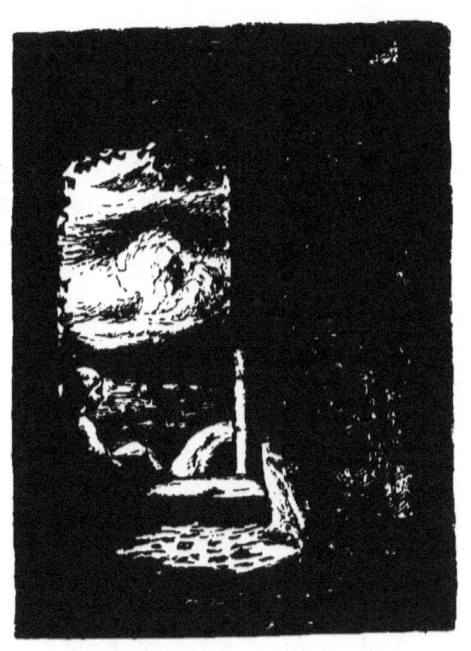

LUCY GRAY;

OR, SOLITUDE.

OFT have I heard of Lucy Gray;
 And, when I crossed the wild,
I chanced to see, at break of day,
 The solitary child.

No mate, no comrade Lucy knew;
 She dwelt on a wide moor,
The sweetest thing that ever grew
 Beside a human door!

FOR THE YOUNG.

"To-night will be a stormy night—
    You to the town must go;
And take a lantern, child, to light
    Your mother through the snow."

"That, father, will I gladly do;
    'Tis scarcely afternoon—
The Minster clock has just struck two,
    And yonder is the moon."

At this the father raised his hook
    And snapped a faggot band;
He plied his work; and Lucy took
    The lantern in her hand.

Not blither is the mountain roe:
    With many a wanton stroke
Her feet disperse the powdery snow,
    That rises up like smoke.

The storm came on before its time:
    She wandered up and down,
And many a hill did Lucy climb,
    But never reached the town.

The wretched parents all that night
  Went shouting far and wide;
But there was neither sound nor sight
  To serve them for a guide.

At daybreak on a hill they stood
  That overlooked the moor,
And thence they saw the bridge of wood,
  A furlong from their door.

FOR THE YOUNG.

You yet may spy the fawn at play,
    The hare upon the green;
But the sweet face of Lucy Gray
    Will never more be seen.

And, turning homeward, now they cried,
    "In heaven we all shall meet!"
When in the snow the mother spied
    The print of Lucy's feet.

Then downward from the steep hill's edge
    They tracked the foot-marks small,
And through the broken hawthorn hedge,
    And by the long stone wall;

And then an open field they crossed:
    The marks were still the same;
They tracked them on, nor ever lost;
    And to the bridge they came.

They followed from the snowy bank
    The foot-marks, one by one,
Into the middle of the plank;
    And farther there were none!

Yet some maintain that to this day
  She is a living child,—
That you may see sweet Lucy Gray
  Upon the lonesome wild.

O'er rough and smooth she trips along,
  And never looks behind;
And sings a solitary song
  That whistles in the wind.

THE SAILOR'S MOTHER.

ONE morning (raw it was and wet,
 A foggy day in winter-time)
A woman on the road I met,
 Not old, though something past her prime;
Majestic in her person, tall and straight,
And like a Roman matron's was her mien and gait.

The ancient spirit is not dead;
 Old times, thought I, are breathing there;
Proud was I that my country bred
 Such strength, a dignity so fair.
She begged an alms, like one in poor estate;
I looked at her again, nor did my pride abate.

When from these lofty thoughts I woke,
 With the first word I had to spare
I said to her, "Beneath your cloak
 What's that which on your arms you bear?"
She answered, soon as she the question heard,
" A simple burthen, Sir,—a little singing-bird."

79

And thus continuing, she said,
   "I had a son, who many a day
   Sailed on the seas: but he is dead;
   In Denmark he was cast away;
And I have travelled far as Hull, to see
What clothes he might have left, or other property.

"The bird and cage they both were his;
   'T was my son's bird; and neat and trim
   He kept it: many voyages
   His singing-bird hath gone with him.
When last he sailed he left the bird behind;
As it might be, perhaps, from bodings of his mind.

"He to a fellow lodger's care
   Had left it to be watched and fed,
   Till he came back again; and there
   I found it when my son was dead;
And now, God help me for my little wit!
I trail it with me, Sir! he took so much delight in it."

ANECDOTE.

I HAVE a boy of five years old;
  His face is fair and fresh to see,
His limbs are cast in beauty's mould;
  And dearly he loves me.

One morn we strolled on our dry walk,
  Our quiet home all full in view,
And held such intermitted talk
  As we are wont to do.

81

My thoughts on former pleasures ran;
  I thought of Kilve's delightful shore,
Our pleasant hope when Spring began,
  A long, long year before.

A day it was when I could bear
  To think—and think—and think again;
With so much happiness to spare,
  I could not feel a pain.

FOR THE YOUNG.

My boy was by my side, so slim
    And graceful in his rustic dress!
And oftentimes I talked to him
    In very idleness.

The young lambs ran a pretty race;
    The morning sun shone bright and warm;
" Kilve," said I, "was a pleasant place,
    And 'so is Liswyn farm.

" My little boy, which like you more,"
    I said, and took him by the arm,—
" Our home by Kilve's delightful shore,
    Or here at Liswyn farm?

" And tell me, had you rather be,"
    I said, and held him by the arm,
" At Kilve's smooth shore by the green sea,
    Or here at Liswyn farm?"

In careless mood he looked at me,
    While still I held him by the arm,
And said, "At Kilve I'd rather be
    Than here at Liswyn farm."

"Now, little Edward, say why so;
  My little Edward, tell me why?"
"I cannot tell, I do not know."
  "Why, this is strange," said I;

"For here are woods and green hills warm:
  There surely must some reason be
That you would change sweet Liswyn farm
  For Kilve by the green sea."

At this my boy hung down his head:
  He blushed with shame, nor made reply;
And five times to the child I said,
  "Why, Edward? tell me why."

His head he raised: there was in sight—
  It caught his eye, he saw it plain—
Upon the house-top, glittering bright,
  A broad and gilded vane.

Then did the boy his tongue unlock;
  And thus to me he made reply:
"At Kilve there was no weathercock,
  And that's the reason why."

FOR THE YOUNG.

O dearest, dearest boy! my heart
  For better lore would seldom yearn,
Could I but teach the hundredth part
  Of what from thee I learn.

THE GREEN LINNET.

BENEATH these fruit-tree boughs that shed
Their snow-white blossoms on my head,
With brightest sunshine round me spread
  Of Spring's unclouded weather,
In this sequestered nook how sweet
To sit upon my orchard seat!
The flowers and birds once more to greet,
  My last year's friends, together.

One have I marked, the happiest guest
In all this covert of the blest:
Hail to thee, far above the rest
  In joy of voice and pinion.
Thou, Linnet, in thy green array,
Presiding spirit here to-day,
Dost lead the revels of the May,
  And this is thy dominion.

While birds, and butterflies, and flowers
Make all one band of paramours,
Thou, ranging up and down the bowers,

FOR THE YOUNG.

Art sole in thy employment:
A life, a presence like the air,
Scattering thy gladness without care,
Too blest with any one to pair,
　　Thyself thy own enjoyment.

Upon yon tuft of hazel trees
That twinkle to the gusty breeze,
Behold him perched in ecstasies,
　　Yet seeming still to hover;
There! where the flutter of his wings
Upon his back and body flings
Shadows and sunny glimmerings,
　　That cover him all over.

While thus before my eyes he gleams,
A brother of the leaves he seems;
When in a moment forth he teems
　　His little song in gushes:
As if it pleased him to disdain
And mock the form which he did feign,
While he was dancing with the train
　　Of leaves among the bushes.

THE COTTAGER TO HER INFANT.

THE days are cold, the nights are long;
The north wind sings a doleful song;
Then hush again upon my breast;
All merry things are now at rest,
   Save thee, my pretty love!

The kitten sleeps upon the hearth,
The crickets long have ceased their mirth;
There's nothing stirring in the house
Save one *wee*, hungry, nibbling mouse;
   Then why so busy thou?

Nay, start not at that sparkling light;
'Tis but the moon that shines so bright
On the window-pane bedropped with rain :
Then, little darling! sleep again,
   And wake when it is day.

TO A SKY-LARK.

Up with me, up with me into the clouds,
 For thy song, Lark, is strong;
Up with me, up with me into the clouds;
  Singing, singing,
 With all the heavens about thee ringing,
Lift me, guide me till I find
That spot which seems so to thy mind.

I have walked through wildernesses dreary,
And to-day my heart is weary;
Had I now the wings of a fairy,
  Up to thee would I fly.
There is madness about thee, and joy divine
  In that song of thine;
Up with me, up with me, high and high,
To thy banqueting-place in the sky!
  Joyous as morning,
  Thou art laughing and scorning:
Thou hast a nest, for thy love and thy rest;
 And, though little troubled with sloth,
 Drunken Lark! thou would'st be loth
To be such a traveller as I.
  Happy, happy liver!
With a soul as strong as a mountain river,
Pouring out praise to the Almighty giver,
 Joy and jollity be with us both!
Hearing thee, or else some other
  As merry a brother,
I on the earth will go plodding on
By myself, cheerfully, till the day is done.

THE RAINBOW.

My heart leaps up when I behold
A Rainbow in the sky:

So was it when my life began;
So is it now I am a man;
So be it when I shall grow old,
    Or let me die!
The child is father of the man;
And I could wish my days to be
Bound each to each by natural piety.

www.ingramcontent.com/pod-product-compliance
Lightning Source LLC
Chambersburg PA
CBHW022149020726
47496CB00008B/2637